Ron Mueller

Burley Bear & Meadow Flower

By: *Ron Mueller*

Around the World Publishing LLC
4914 Cooper Road Suite 144
Cincinnati, Ohio 45242-9998

ISBN 13: 978-1-68223-215-6
ISBN 10: 1-68223-215-8

Distributed by Ingram
Cover Design By: Ron Mueller
Cover Picture By: Hien Mueller

ಬಿ Dedicated to
All those who are different,
committed and strong.

Burley Bear, Meadow Flower

The stand of massive, tall straight pines provided Burley Bear shade and the luxury of relaxing as he recovered from having hoisted four massive buffalo into the trees. Meadow Flower sat next to him on the body of an ancient pine that had lost its hold on the earth. As it fell it had ripped the limbs off the younger surrounding trees. It left a streak of the blue sky to testify to the path the giant pine had taken on its way down.

He wondered how loud such a fall would have been. He took note of the breeze entering from the edge of the forest and rising past him on its way upward through the opening above. The opening provided a natural path for the wind.

He thought back to the oddity of how his current clan had come to be. It was made up of the unification of many small three and four family clans that had banded together after an especially hard and devastating winter. Prior to that winter the various small clans had been spread out so each small clan could hunt uncontested in their territory.

This had work for thousands of moon cycles. Then the loss of almost half of the small clan groups to an extremely cold and snow driven season had caused this practice to change.

His clan and about ten handful of other clans had come together. The combined clans moved across vast snow-covered territory and had ended making their primary camp in a green trench valley to the east of their current location.

It was during this period when their current seer, Broken Spear had earned his name. He had been mauled by a huge bear that had left him with many broken bones and a disfigured face.

He had been broken but he had been given new powers by the ancients. His new powers included flying with the birds and seeing through their eyes.

Burley Bear was just a youngster when Broken Spear had predicted that a man of the eagle would come to lead the clan to a new home. It was many moons later that he and the clan again faced a devastating winter. They were barely keeping all the families fed.

It was in the beginning of that winter when Broken Spear told the clan that they should go to the ocean shore and wait for the man of the eagle to guide them to a new home.

It was a crazy time to make such a move. Burley Bear made his voice heard but Quiet Fox his father and the leader of the clan listened to Broken Spear.

The clan moved to a perilous location by the sea.

Burley Bear's scouting led him to a camp of the new ones that was processing a large amount of meat. Somehow the leader of the hunt group sensed his presence.

Later when he led a team to take the meat from the new ones, they tricked him by loading the travois they pulled with wood and a small amount of meat.

He became the laughingstock of the old hunters and they asked him if he could tell the difference between wood and meat.

A few suns later he watched as a travois pulled by two women of the new ones and two young boys approached the clan. They came with gifts of some small goods and more meat than he had taken from the four travois his team had captured.

He had not meant to be rude, but the strength of his grip was more than he meant it to be when he grabbed the woman with the white feather in her hair.

The next thing he remembered was awakening in his hutch. He knew immediately that an unseen warrior had blind-sided him. He came out of his hutch roaring and ready to fight.

Instead of the pandemonium and fighting that he had expected, he found Quiet Fox talking to the taller of the two young men.

As he approached the young man stood up.

At the same time an eagle let out a loud scream overhead.

There was total silence as the young man introduced himself as the claw of the eagle.

The claw of the eagle, Taelo, had defended his mother and put out his lights. He had done what no other person in the clan had ever been able to do.

He had overcome Burley Bear.

The eagle passed overhead and let out another scream.

Burley Bear took it was a signal to him. He apologized to Taelo's mother and shook Taelo's hand.

Then in another surprise, Quiet Fox asked for him to be Taelo's defender and look out for him.

In time, his relationship with Taelo an Golden Hawk became so close that he now thought of them as brothers.

After that it seemed that good things just kept happening.

Taelo led them to a whale on the beach.

Next, he found a home for the clan that included a warm water pool.

Then on a journey where the three of them moved into manhood together, they found the valley of plenty where a sea of buffalo wintered.

Then in the spring they put up a fish trap that yielded enough fish for both the Elk Clan and his clan that was referred to by the new ones as the Clan of Others.

Taelo had invited the Clan of Others to participate in harvesting the fish from the fish trap.

Taelo's father, Grey Fox Running, Taelo's father had invited the clan of Others to attend the late season meeting of all the Elk sub-clans.

The teeth from a giant shark they caught in their fish trap and the salt they made from the sea water made all of them very well to do young men.

Then White Swan and Quiet Pheasant had arranged for the current long hunt he and the team were on. It was her attempt to change the culture of her clan and raise the status of women in her clan.

It was hard to keep up with the events that surrounded Taelo.

He felt Meadow Flower's hand as she ran it down his shoulder. Her action brought him out of his reminiscing. He watched Taelo and Quiet Rabbit slowly cull out the mother buffalo and the very late young calf. He knew Taelo had some ulterior motive for rescuing the young calf, but it escaped him what it might be.

Meadow Flower asked him why Taelo had not spoken up about killing four buffalo when Little Otter was boasting about Golden Hawk's success at killing four buffalo.

In fact, Taelo had not only killed four buffalo but had dropped each of them so close to the forest that their team's processing was almost done when Golden Hawk's first buffalo was hoisted into the trees.

He replied to her question by making the point that Taelo was completely confident in himself and did not seek the compliments of others. He pointed out that Golden Hawk had the same attitude.

He made the observation that the two were complements of each other.

He jumped up as he watched Taelo take the young calf down and tie its feet. He was momentarily afraid the mother buffalo was going to attack but then he watched Quiet Rabbit bravely jump up with her spear in one hand and a piece of leather in the other. Her action stopped the mother buffalo and it retreated as Quiet Rabbit continued her advance.

He commented to Meadow Flower that the mother buffalo could have easily run over Quiet Rabbit had it been more aggressive.

Meadow Flower responded that Quiet Rabbit would have knelt and placed the spear to the buffalo's chest.

She had half expected her to have killed the ninth buffalo. She pointed out that not only was Quiet Rabbit, brave she was fast, and she had learned a new and deadly skill.

After Taelo returned with the young buffalo and tied it to one of the trees. He went over to where Golden Hawk's team was still processing their kill.

Burley Bear went with Taelo and together they pulled in the other three buffalo that Golden Hawk had killed.

Golden Hawk almost immediately noted and complemented Taelo on his success and thanked him for his help.

This exchange had stopped Little Otter in mid-sentence as he realized that Taelo had also killed four buffalo and the work of processing those four was done.

Meadow Flower commented that eight buffalo far exceeded her expectation of how successful they would be. She said that it was hard for her to believe that anyone could run as fast as either Taelo or Golden Hawk. She had been amazed that Quiet Rabbit and Busy Bee had both kept up and had been able to carry the extra spears.

She commented on the fact that she was stronger than any of the new ones, but she certainly would never be able to move as fast as they did.

Burley Bear jokingly commented that she only had to run fast enough to catch him, and he would make sure he always ran slow enough to get caught.

Meadow Flower thought back to only a few sun's ago, when she had been surprised when Broken Spear, the Clan's seer approached her and told her that she should prepare to go on a long hunt with a long hunt group made up of the new ones and Burley Bear. He explained that the group was a mix of young men and women. These young men and women did not know it, but this long hunt would bond them for life.

Each would find a mate.

He saw her as the mate for Burley Bear.

Meadow Flower laughed and told Broken Spear that a seer was not needed to make the connection between her and Burley Bear. The two of them were life-long friends and had promised to be one another's mate when they were only eight seasons old. Every year the two of them would walk through the forest holding hands. They would comment on having passed another cycle of seasons and discuss what they had learned. They would again verify that they still were on track to spend all the coming seasons together.

She stopped and thanked Broken Spear for having crystalized the situation and for making the bond official. This would make it easy for her father Quiet Fox to accept Burley Bear. He had always questioned her devotion and belief in him.

Quiet Rabbit's groan as she followed Taelo and the young calf into the forest brought Meadow Flower back to the present.

She took the two spears Quiet Rabbit was carrying and took her over to the fire where she had a piece of the buffalo hump roasting.

It was clear to her that Quiet Rabbit had used the last bit of her energy to go out with Taelo.

During the race to determine who would be put on each team, she had watched Quiet Rabbit accelerate and pass Busy Bee and Talking Wren as if they were standing still. It was clear to her who Taelo's mate was to be.

She realized that race had been at the beginning of this sun cycle and Quiet Rabbit had been going full steam for the entire time.

She put stamina on the list of things the two different clans had in common.

Burley Bear followed Taelo. He went out with Taelo and helped him bring two long branches to make into a heavy-duty travois. The two branches would easily carry a buffalo.

He let out a little laugh of disbelief when Taelo told him the travois was for the young buffalo he had captured.

He soon swallowed that same a laugh when Taelo began to make a harness like the one Burley Bear had made for the three of them to pull the sled with three buffalo on it.

He realized and was amazed that Taelo had extrapolated the idea of harnessing a human to a sled to doing so with a buffalo.

The young buffalo fought the arrangement but by the time the sun was ready to descent behind the far mountains Taelo, and Little Otter had pulled four buffalo and hung them just outside of their main campsite.

While the meat was being pulled in, Burley Bear and Golden Hawk arranged a pen that would hold the young buffalo. They agreed that the young buffalo deserved to be guarded.

They were relieved when Little Otter and Talking Wren volunteered to stay up and guard it.

Burley Bear was not sure he could have stayed awake to properly guard anything. He barely had the energy to climb up into his sleeping area in the tree.

The young buffalo proved to be invaluable. Burley Bear, Meadow Flower, Quiet Rabbit and Busy Bee processed and packaged most of the meat while Taelo, Golden Hawk and Little Otter brought the meat in. The last load included a young boar that Golden Hawk had surprised and killed.

Marigold excused herself from the processing of the last buffalo and proceeded to prepare the young boar for a celebration dinner.

During the celebration dinner the team decided that they should send the first load of meat back to both the Cave of the Others and the Elk Camp.

Little Otter volunteered to take the meat back. He claimed the young bull was attached to him.

Burley Bear had a good laugh when he learned that Little Otter had named the young bull Little Burley after himself and Burley Bear. Little Otter claimed the young bull had demonstrated the strength of both of them.

When Talking Wren volunteered to accompany Little Otter, Marigold commented that would mean the hunters would have some peace and quiet.

She kept quiet as Quiet Rabbit commented that Talking Wren's company would follow Taelo's rule of always having a partner during the hunt. It was clear to her that the whole team agreed and looked forward to a few days of quiet.

The two hunt teams continued to hunt. Marigold went with Golden Hawk and Burley Bear continued to support Taelo.

Burley Bear commented that Taelo and Golden Hawk had changed their focus to hunting a more diverse mix of animals.

They were bringing in many deer, elk, wild boar, and a host of smaller game.

Meadow Flower agreed but pointed out that the quantity still exceeded what she had expected. It appeared to her that by the time Little Otter returned it would be time to send a second load of meat back to both clans.

A few sun cycles later a long hunter from her clan came into camp with the news that a crazed saber tooth tiger had attacked his team.

He announced that Rolling Stone had been slashed across the chest and might not make i.

Meadow Flower reacted with emotion. Rolling Stone was a friend. He was to her sister what Burley Bear was to her.

Rolling Stone was a friend of Burley Bear and he would have left immediately had Taelo not intervened.

It was dark. There was no moon. If a saber tooth tiger was out then they would be easy targets.

Taelo suggested letting the long hunt messenger get a good night sleep and, in the morning, the entire team would go to rescue the other long hunters.

That night Burley Bear awoke to the putrid smell of death. It was very early in the morning and the sun was threatening to rise over the far distant mountains.

Suddenly an ear-splitting roar came from where Taelo had his sleeping area.

With spear in hand, Burley Bear jumped down from his sleeping area. He watched as Taelo recovered from his fall out of the tree. Taelo's spear was lying next to a monstrous saber tooth tiger that was also recovering from the fall.

Burley Bear began shouting and whooping in an attempt to distract the tiger.

He watched as Taelo also began yelling and then turned and ran out of camp. The saber tooth seemed to reject him and went after Taelo.

Burley Bear followed the two. He was yelling as loudly as possible in hopes of distracting the saber tooth.

He watched as the saber tooth slowly closed the gap to Taelo. He was not sure if Taelo would make it to the lake.

Burley Bear was shocked when Quiet Rabbit passed him as she yelled at the top of her voice. He watched as she slowly closed the gap to the tiger and Taelo.

He wondered what she would do when she caught up. He could not keep pace. It was clear to him that Quiet Rabbit was very likely to catch up with Taelo and the tiger.

He had arrived and found a bewildered Quiet Rabbit that was frantically calling for Taelo.

For a short period, they could not locate Taelo.

Burley Bear thanked the ancients for Taelo's miraculous survival. He and the tiger fell down into a water filled chimney hole.

Taelo had found an alternate way out but the dead tiger was floating down in the water.

Quiet Rabbit volunteered to be lowered into the dark chimney and tie a rope to tiger. This cemented Burley Bear's opinion that she had to be one of the bravest persons he had ever met.

The rise of the sun gave light to the morning as he, Meadow Flower and the lead hunter of the Others lifted the tiger from the shaft.

He then dropped the rope back down into the dark shaft and single handedly pulled Quiet Rabbit out of the shaft.

Once the tiger was hanging in the tree, Burley bear led the team to rescue his friend.

He was shocked at the condition that he found Rolling Stone. The five deep slashes of the tiger across his chest exposed the chest bones.

His first reaction was to wish his friend a smooth way to the ancients.

He pulled Marigold out of the way and stepped back as Quiet Rabbit knelt next to Rolling Stone.

She carefully examined each slash. Then she washed out the wound with salt and water mixture.

She then coated each slash with honey.

She carefully arranged the flaps of skin and flesh.

Then she stitched the deep part of each slash wound. She began with the gut thread knots on the outside and ended the inner stitching with the end also knotted to the outside.

Finally, he watched her stitch the top of the gash, so the edges were just touching each other. He made the observation that the scars would heal with a smooth exterior.

Meadow Flower watched Quiet Rabbit and asked about each step. She asked where Quiet Rabbit had learned how to treat such cuts.

Quiet Rabbit thought for a moment and said that she had learned to clean wounds from her mother and good sewing techniques from her grandmother. She had put them together for the first time when she saw the wounds on Rolling Stones chest.

She had figured out how to make sure the thread for the deep stitches could be pulled out by watching Taelo and Golden Hawk handle their ropes during their cliff climbing during the spring egg gathering.

Meadow Flower looked up at Burley Bear, raised one eyebrow and quietly commented that maybe she should not have asked.

Rolling Stone opened his eyes. He asked where he was. When asked how he felt, he commented that he felt better.

Quiet Rabbit put her hand to his chest and told him he was safe; the tiger was dead, and he would get the best care. She told him that sleep was the best medicine.

Rolling Stone seemed to relax and fall asleep.

Burley Bear had the entire long hunt team of the Others return to the cave. He assured them that the clan would have all the meat they would need, and they should recover and then make sure Rolling Stone got what he needed.

He knew that the Valley of Plenty had a wealth of buffalo and this long hunt was one that White Swan and Silent Pheasant had used to enhance the standing of women in the Elk Clan.

Two sun cycles later, Meadow Flower looked up the valley to the water cascading down the cliff and the steam rising from the warm water pool. She was leading the hunt team back. She planned to explain the care that her sister Marigold was to give to Rolling Stone and then she would return to the hunt.

Quiet Rabbit had insisted she accompany Rolling Stone back to the cave.

Taelo had agreed and highlighted the safety factor and that there should always be two traveling together.

Meadow Flower had agreed. Her main concern was to get Rolling Stone back to the safety and the care he would get at the cave.

Marigold was startled by the pale look on Rolling Stone's face.

Broken Spear looked at the wound and complimented Quiet Rabbit when he found out she had sealed the gashes. He commented on the excellent repair work she had done on Rolling Stone and said that had she been around when the bear mauled him, he might have been much better looking.

He went on to state that Rolling Stone, like himself had earned a new name. He would be called Saber Scar for the marks on his chest.

Meadow Flower and Quiet Rabbit enjoyed the hot pool and a solid relaxed, night's rest. At sunrise they packed their gear and started their journey back to the area they expected to find the long hunt team.

They arrived to find the camp had been cleared and a stone signal pointed the way to where the team was heading.

Quiet Rabbit became anxious when she saw the drawing of a mastodon in the dirt by the stone marker.

She stepped up the pace to catch up to Taelo.

Burley Bear was surprised by Taelo's decision to move. He had come back with the news of a very large mastodon herd that he wanted to follow.

When the team decided to kill one mastodon, he knew that the hunt team would set a record for the amount of meat a long hunt team would bring back.

Taelo and Golden Hawk pointed to the fact that bringing back the meat of a mastodon would be a first for the Elk Clan. They also pointed out that their long hunt team would be breaking all records for the amount of meat brought in.

Their plan was to follow the herd but only bag deer, elk, boar, and any other small animal they came across.

They would hunt the mastodon when Meadow Flower and Quiet Rabbit returned. This would allow the entire team to participate in what might be a once in a lifetime experience.

Two sun cycles passed before Burley Bear spotted two joggers approaching. The pair made up of a large jogger and one that was smaller than her shadow at the sun's zenith could only be Quiet Rabbit and his Meadow Flower.

He called for a stop and began putting together a cooking ring. He put pieces of boar meat on a spit, salted it and put it over the hot coals.

He had praised Taelo for the decision to wait on hunting the mastodon. Now as he watched the two joggers, he felt the team would be successful.

Quiet Rabbit commented to Meadow Flower that the hunt team had stopped early. Meadow Flower replied that she was sure Burley Bear had spotted them and made the call to stop.

Quiet Rabbit was surprised by the salted boar and roasted onion dinner. She complemented Burley Bear for being so quick and so good at having something to eat.

His smile, which always reminded her of a grimace, was indication that he liked the compliment.

The next sunrise Taelo, Golden Hawk and Quiet Rabbit set out to select a young bull mastodon. It did not surprise him when Quiet Rabbit returned to lead the team to where Taelo and Golden Hawk were to guide a single mastodon.

She was anxious that the team leave as early the next sunrise as possible. She was worried that Taelo and Golden Hawk might not be able to wait on the whole team.

Burley Bear reassured her that Taelo would wait for the whole team to participate.

He and Meadow flower were again impressed at Taelo's and Golden Hawks ingenuity when they saw the trap that the two had devised to capture a mastodon.

He and his clan had hunted mastodon before. Their hunt style required a cliff that they could run the mastodon over. Another more dangerous technique was to surround the animal and wear it out by repeatedly making it rear up by attacking it.

He lauded Taelo and Golden Hawk for having successfully trapped the mastodon into a tight, steep sided ravine.

He felt especially honored when he was asked to be the one to spear the animal through the heart.

He almost dropped his spear when on the other side of the ravine, Little Otter slipped and started to slide down into the ravine.

He watched as Talking Wren grabbed Little Otter's hair and pulled him back up the slope.

He plunged his spear just behind and above the front leg of the mastodon. Meadow Flower who had taken Little Otter's spear did the same from the other side.

He and the rest of the team let out a shout as the mastodon went down on its knees. It had died almost immediately.

Burley Bear decided that each hunting technique had it good and its bad. Getting the mastodon back out of the ravine took much more effort than any of the team had anticipated.

Their share of the long hunt would be more than any team hunters of Others had ever harvested. He and Meadow Flower would be among the most prolific long hunters in their clan's verbal history.

The travois pulled by the young buffalo made it possible to pull all the meat and choice pieces of the mastodon. Their additional meat and numerous hides were pulled on three travois by two team members on each travois.

Burley Bear and Meadow Flower were always on separate travois. He thanked Taelo for having arranged it so the two of them could walk together during their break from pulling.

He shared with her the fact that he had celebrated throughout the night when he had found out that she was to accompany him as his hunting partner. The fact that Broken Spear had announced this long hunt made up of paired mates had saved him from having to ask Quiet Fox for her hand.

Meadow Flower asked if as big as he was, was he afraid of her father.

He replied that he was not afraid of him but of his possible rejection. Such a position would have forced his hand.

Meadow Flower stopped and gave Burley Bear a hug.

Taelo stopped at the same time and commented that he thought only Burley Bear's mother loved him enough to hug him.

Burley Bear laughed and agreed that for a long time he had thought the same thing.

He then pointed to Meadow Flower and said she had given him her friendship and the confidence to weather all challenges.

Soon, Burley Bear went with the Elk Clan as the Clan of Others joined together to attend the cycle gathering in the valley where the eagle and Broken Spear had first watched the very young Taelo, standing on the naming hide, holding up the eagle's claw.

He was aware that the two clans had arrived early in order to set up camp on the far side of the lake. The presence of the Others at the Elk Clan gathering was certain to raise many questions and certainly some objections.

At the first meeting of the Elk Clan council, he listened to the eloquent description Grey Fox Running gave of the Clan of Others. He went on to describe the role of women in the Clan of Others and that the Elk Clan had elected White Swan, Quiet Pheasant and Floating Cloud to the Elk Clan leadership council. This raised numerous objections.

Grey Fox Running, named Golden Hawk, Taelo and himself as hunters of the clan. Taelo's and Golden Hawk's age gave rise to a host of objections.

Quite Fox announced that his clan had also made both of them hunters in the Clan of Others.

Wise Owl, the overall leader for the meeting had to ask for silence. He made that point that the Elk Clan had left the last meeting in a desperate situation. In one season they had returned with wealth that exceeded that of all the other clans put together.

He pointed to the salt, the fish, the buffalo meat and hides that were freely being distributed to each clan. He asked that all the Elk sub-clan leaders should think about what this meant and what message the Ancients were trying to send to them.

He, Taelo and Golden Hawk were in the dark outside of the meeting area. They commented on the power that Wise Owl had just demonstrated. They knew they had made a significant contribution to the direction of all the Elk Clans.

On the return to the Elk Camp by the seashore, Taelo described a trip to the south, a trip that he offered to all the members of the hunt team.

There was an immediate acceptance. The team wanted to have another experience together.

The Long hunt had bonded them.

A new adventure, Burley Bear was sure, would give them a new reason for tightening that bond.

He would follow Taelo anywhere.

He and Meadow Flower were where they wanted to be.

The End

Thank you for reading to this point!

The Stories of Taelo are set in the distant past, long before the time currently given as to when people migrated into the western hemisphere.

This is purposely done since the stories are meant to engage the reader in a story and not relate exact history.

The adventures of Taelo and Golden Hawk provide the backdrop for stories featuring the values of treating others as you wish to be treated, of responsibility, integrity, honesty and of contribution, and the joy of learning.

About the Author
Ronald E. Mueller
remwriter95@gmail.com
Ron grew up in what is now Flint River State Park in Southeast Iowa. The 170-year-old house Ron lived in is built into a hillside. It faces a 125-foot-high cliff towering over the little Flint River. The house and the land talked to him about; the passing of time, the struggle to conquer the land, the struggles people faced and the wonder of nature.

He climbed the cliffs, crawled into the caves, dove from the swimming rock, collected clams from the bottom of the pond, gigged and skinned frogs for their legs. He trapped muskrats for fur, hunted raccoon in the dead of night, and with only a stick hunted rabbits in the dead of winter.

His young life was outdoors, and nature tested him.

He walked to a one room: stone schoolhouse uphill both ways. A stern but warm-hearted teacher, Mrs. Henry was instrumental in shaping his character as she shepherded him from the fourth to the eighth grade. A Montessori before its time. It was a great way to grow up.

His experiences inter-twined with snippets of fantasy lend themselves to the adventures Taelo leads the reader through.

Ron has told many similar stories to impart life values and influence the thinking of his children and now grandchildren. He feels stories are a wonderful means for parents and their children to engage in meaningful discussions about behavior and fundamental values and principles.

A Taelo Story:
    The Name of the Child
    White Swan and Quiet Pheasant
    Broken Spear
    Floating Cloud
    Quiet Rabbit
    Busy Bee
    Little Otter and Talking Wren
    Burley Bear, Meadow Flower

If you enjoyed the stories, try:

The Taelo Series by Ron Mueller
    Taelo: The Early Years
    Taelo: The Golden Feather
    Taelo: Journey of Discovery
    Taelo: Dangerous Passage
    Taelo: Condor Clan Slingers

Other books by Around the World Publishing
Science Fiction Books by Ron Mueller
    The Door Series:
      The Door
      Delivery
      Journey Beyond
    The Savitar Series:
      Journey's End
      Savitar
      Confluence
    Current Past and Future
    Event Survivors
Fiction Books by Ron Mueller
    The Problem Solver Series:
      The Early Years
      Drug Lords
      Border Crossers
    The Alex Evercrest Series
      The River Front
      Girl on the Grill
      Missing
      Maggot
Imagination by Courtney Huynh &
        Chloe Parker

Published by: Around the World Publishing LLC.

QR Links to
ATWP.US web site

www.ingramcontent.com/pod-product-compliance
Lightning Source LLC
Chambersburg PA
CBHW060602100726
47907CB00005B/1480